The SWEET DREAMS Book

By Alida Allison
Illustrations by Laurie Gray

PRICE/STERN/SLOAN
Publishers, Inc., Los Angeles
1984

Also by Alida Allison:

THE POTTY BOOK
THE CHILDREN'S MANNERS BOOK

ISBN: 0-8431-1037-6

A Note to Parents
about Sweet Dreams

What we have on our minds as we're falling asleep affects how well we sleep and the kinds of dreams we have. Worries, rages, sadnesses—these are the stuff of nightmares. Sweet dreams are anti-nightmares. And to encourage anti-nightmares, we can use the power of the subconscious mind to receive images; positive images tend to produce peaceful sleep. This is as true for children as it is for adults. *The Sweet Dreams Book* fosters anti-nightmares by planting peaceful images—verbal and visual—in the fertile time before sleep.

Through the night sweet dreams I'll see:
Ten thousand things that I can be.

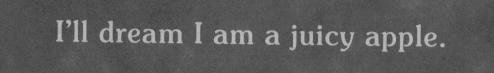

I'll dream I am a juicy apple.

I'll dream I am a bright red rose.

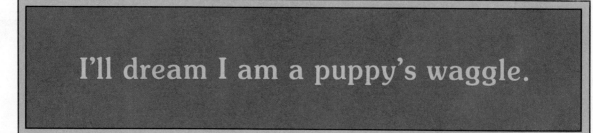

I'll dream I am a puppy's waggle.

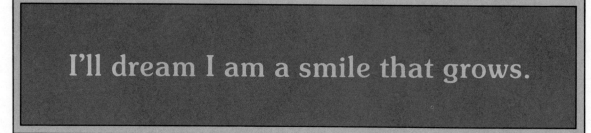

I'll dream I am a smile that grows.

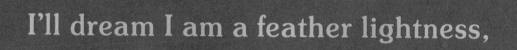

I'll dream I am a feather lightness,

Dream I am a starry brightness,

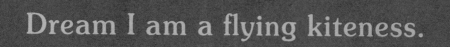

Dream I am a flying kiteness.

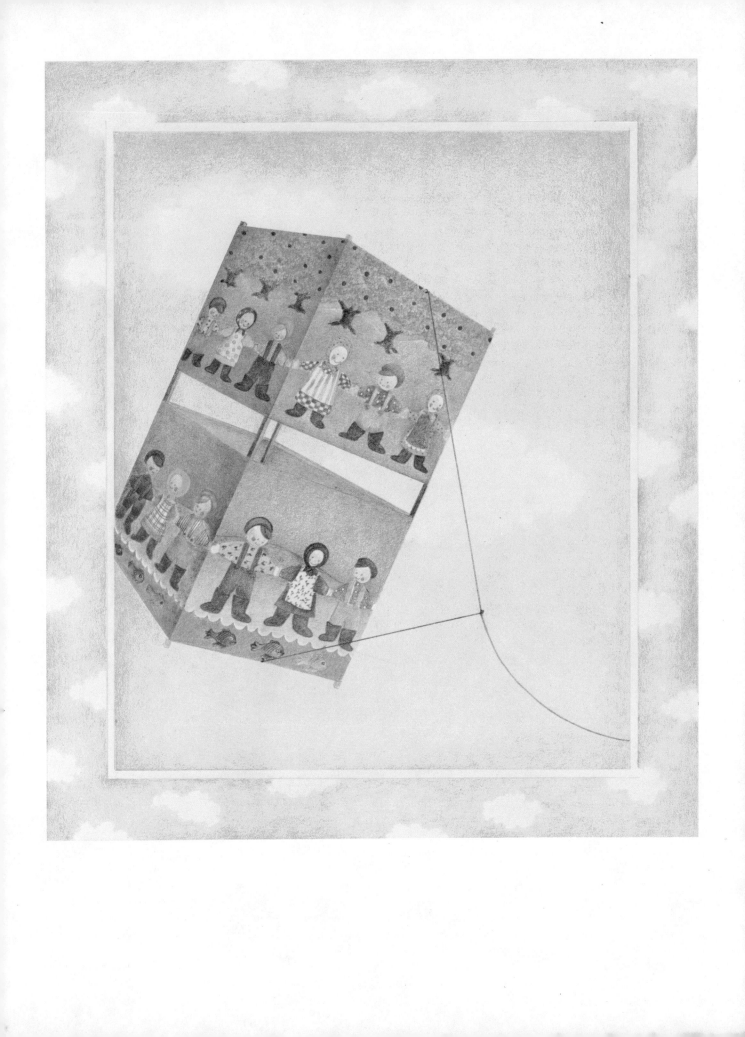

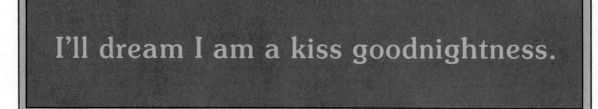

I'll dream I am a kiss goodnightness.

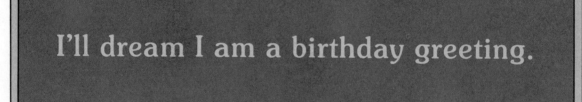

I'll dream I am a birthday greeting.

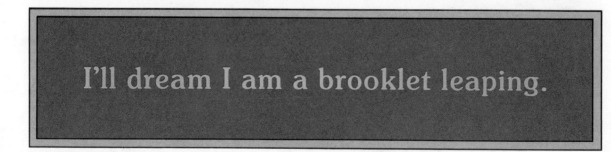

I'll dream I am a brooklet leaping.

I'll dream I am a kitten eating.

I'll dream I am a baby sleeping.

But best of all, so cozily,
I will dream that I am ME!